LETHAL INTERACTION

by

Nick Papakyriakopoulos

1

Arthur opened the door of his silver-coloured electric car and got out, slowly but steadily. He was not drunk, although he had four vodkas in the three hours he spent tonight at DE LORENZO'S . He was proud of his ability to hold his liquor. So far, it has proved useful, especially at business lunches. After the third glass of the expensive French wine, Arthur always used to order, the other guy turned careless and started talking. Arthur spared his company and his career a lot of bad deals, by listening carefully to his lunch companion, and detecting a possible lack of profit or some trouble he might encounter in his future business transactions.

Tonight, he left Susan's apartment at two-thirty, after forty five minutes of wild sex and soothing spooning afterwards. She was sleeping when he left, and he had stood for a moment in the doorway, admiring her beautiful naked body, all sweaty and glittering under the dim light, her left thigh, only half covered by the silk sheets.

Half an hour later, when he slipped his magnetic key card into the electronic lock of his 12th floor apartment he remembered that he did not switch on his car-alarm.

"The garage is perfectly safe", he thought to himself, "but I'll turn it on anyway."

He headed to the elevator, starting to feel how tired he was and looking forward to the fact that he would be upstairs again at no time. As the elevator doors opened at the garage level, he caught a glimpse of a human shadow just behind his car and next to a black limousine, at the far end of the dark garage.   It was a female figure, standing in the shadows.

"Anybody there?", he called, approaching carefully to his car. There was no response. Arthur heard nothing and saw nothing as he got closer to the spot where he thought he saw the figure.

"It was probably my imagination", Arthur switched on the alarm and walked back to the elevator.

At the morning, after having a quick cup of coffee, Arthur drove to the office. The streaming platform guys from Brazil were again all over his texts, having some of their usual ridiculous requests. After dealing with them, he e-mailed Paris to close the deal with the French movies on-demand site. His schedule as the top marketing executive of G&G FILMS Inc. began every morning at nine o'clock and usually kept him at the office until late in the afternoon. Today he had his lunch with an English film promotion agency executive, trying to talk him into, proposing to the board meeting of his company to handle G&G FILMS' North-Western Europe advertising.

The outcome of the lunch was not successful and Arthur, a little upset, drove back to his apartment to have a tranquilliser. He didn't keep any at his office to prevent himself from taking the pills frequently. As he drove into the garage, he was thinking of how unreasonably he behaved, because he always drove home when he needed one.

Two police cars were parked in the garage along with an ambulance with their lights flashing. Some policemen were questioning the garage guy and two paramedics were collecting something that looked like a dead body. Arthur got out of his car and asked them what was going on. He saw what appeared to be the body of a brutally murdered young woman. He was told that it was the third time during this week that a murder of that kind was taking place. The murderer, all three times, killed young women during night hours by tearing off the skin from all over their body, using some kind of a razor. Arthur was asked if he had seen anyone, when he parked his car the other night. He said that he didn't, and told them that he hoped they would catch the killer. As he was going upstairs to his apartment, Arthur did not gave a second thought to the fact that he hadn't told them anything about catching a glimpse of that female figure the other night. He was positive that it must have been his imagination.

2

Susan slightly lifted her tight leather skirt as she walked into Arthur's car.   Arthur smiled to himself, thinking of the night ahead of them, at Susan's apartment. They were going for dinner at an expensive French restaurant, that Susan had heard about and was looking forward on trying it. As she was talking about her day and how she spent the most boring three hours of her life listening to the chattering of an Italian rich old lady at the hairdresser's, Arthur was reconsidering the deal he blew today with the English executive and how he would make it up by arranging something with a major American movie maker and distributor.

"Yes", he tried to convince himself, "it was not such a dreadful loss." The incident in the garage, and the dead body of the young woman did not upset him at all. He just pushed the thought back, into the far ends of his mind, as something unimportant that would only shadow his, otherwise, easy going life.

His life was going quite well. He was only thirty-two years old, had a great executive job which made him lots of money, a beautiful and sexy girlfriend, a luxurious uptown apartment, an expensive electric car. He had it all.

Or so he thought.

Arthur was washing down the last bite of Les Escargots Sautés with his fourth glass of Chateau Bollinger as he was listening to Susan describing him a new club some friend told her about. She said that they had to go and check it out, after dinner. Arthur agreed and nodded to the waiter, asking for the bill.

"Tonight, we 're really gonna have fun and forget about everything else", he said to Susan and got a hold of her soft, warm hands.   Susan smiled to him and rose immediately as soon as Arthur swiped his phone against the POS.

Arthur stepped heavily on the accelerator and the car raced down the driveway of the restaurant, leaving behind a sense of urgency.

"Are we going to the MERGER CLUB Arthur?" Susan asked, as the car entered the highway.

"How do we get there?"

"Turn left at the next traffic lights and we'll see the sign. That's what Mary told me... Hey, guess what I heard at the news today! There was a body found at the garage of **your** apartment building. It was some kind of a maniac taking off the skin of those poor girls with a razor..."

"Yes, I saw the police asking questions. But don't think about it tonight, Suz. Tonight, we are having fun!"

At MERGER CLUB, Arthur had a couple of strong whiskeys and danced with Susan, who was very excited and enthusiastic about the club.

She had two vodkas, and soon became quite drunk and started throwing herself over to Arthur as they danced. Arthur took her by the waist and they were soon inside the car, driving back to Susan's apartment.

While they were still in the car, Susan started unbuttoning her blouse, very slowly, and gave Arthur her familiar promising look. As soon as they got to the apartment, he watched her kicking off her shoes and zipping down her skirt with playful moves. Arthur loosened his tie and followed her to the bedroom.

3

Susan woke up and opened her eyes to check the time at the phone, by her bed. It was too early to get up. She didn't have to get to work on time anyway, as her boss was also her lover. She was the secretary of the chief marketing executive of G&G FILMS and she had a salary that allowed her to rent an expensive, luxurious apartment and live quite comfortably. Arthur paid for every other wish she had. He was always very generous and Susan was grateful for all his expensive gifts. Arthur was also a great lover, the best she's had for quite some time. She could only compare him to her high school sweetheart, an athlete and a motorcycle racer, the first man she was truly in love with. Susan was not quite sure if she was in love with Arthur. She certainly enjoyed having sex with him, but she never felt that she was in love with him. She was not worried about it though, as she was having a good time and felt that she was happy.

The car stereo in Susan's red convertible was playing one of her favourite tunes when she stepped gently on the brakes, getting closer to a red light. It was then, when she caught a glimpse of breaking news, flashing on the screen of her phone.

"Razor Killer's New Victim" and just below it, with smaller letters "Near Merger Club".

"I was there with Arthur just yesterday", she was thinking as she accelerated when the green light flashed.

"I'm sure we'll come to an understanding when we meet next Thursday... Yes, Mr. Palmer... Thank you so much... I'll see you then." Arthur hang up the phone with a smile on his face. He had just arranged a meeting with an executive of the American film company to discuss a possible cooperation with G&G FILMS.

His company had lead a quite successful marketing strategy, for the last two years, thanks to Arthur being head of the marketing department. Arthur was very proud of his work in G&G but always aimed at new, more promising and certainly more profitable jobs in bigger corporations. After closing the deal with the Americans he was planning to have a discrete look for a potential position for himself in the American film corporation's marketing department.

He would entertain Mr. Palmer, the American executive, become friends with him, and eventually gain his confidence. Then he would get all the information he needed about his corporation. Arthur, had his way with people, and got everybody to like him. Mr. Palmer was unlikely to be an exception.

Arthur started typing on his instant messaging app to call his secretary.

"Miss Faithwell, could you come in for a minute?" his fingers scrolled down the screen.

"Right away, sir." Susan replied adding a smiley emoji, and got into Arthur's office, straightening her silk, black stockings.

Arthur smiled as she saw her coming in, and he asked with a half-serious, half-humorous tone, "Are you free for lunch today, Miss Faithwell?"

"But of course, Mr. Twines", Susan sat on Arthur's lap, trying to cover a giggle.

4

Susan was ready to take a bath, being really tired after her day at the office. As she was getting into the hot tab the phone rang. "No, no, I'm not answering it", she said to herself, welcoming the hot water all over her body. The phone kept ringing and Susan thought that it must be Arthur. "OK, I'll answer it, it might be important", she tried to convince her body to leave the hot tab.

"Hello", Susan answered the phone, without looking at the screen, in an impatient almost angry voice.

Nobody replied at the other end of the line.

"Hello, is that you Arthur?"

She heard nothing but a strange sound that she could not exactly make out. After a few more seconds of that weird, scratching-like sound Susan shouted angrily, "All-right you pervert, I hang up." There was no caller-id and it sure wasn't Arthur who called her.

Susan returned to her tab, really furious for being interrupted for nothing. Then the phone rang again. No caller-id again but she decided to answer anyway.

"If you keep doing that I'll call the cops..."

"What's that? Is that you Susan?" a woman's voice asked.

"Kathy! I'm sorry dear! A pervert called a few seconds back and kept doing some strange sounds..."

"Don't worry Susan. It happens to everyone. The world is full of them."

"I'm not worried, just angry. He got me out of my hot bath!"

The young woman was crossing the park to get to her apartment building. She was late and it was getting dark. Her car had broken down, for the second time this month, and she had to walk home again. The park was quiet and she only heard her own heist footsteps. She was too anxious to get out of the unfriendly dark surroundings and she didn't notice the figure of a man, hiding in the shadows behind her.

As she took a first glimpse of the street lights at the end of the path, leading to the exit, she sighed with relief. This relief however, gave way to fear when she heard some heavy footsteps coming towards her from behind. She didn't dare to look back and she tried to run to the gate. The stranger's strong grasp caught her foot and pulled her back violently, dropping her on the moist ground. She didn't have the chance to release her desperate scream, that was struggling to come out, as the man stuffed a piece of cloth in her mouth. She tried to kick the man and desperately reached for the branches from the trees around her. It was of no use. The man kept dragging her on the ground, and to the dark bushes. After a few agonizing minutes the throttling sound of the leaves stopped. It was followed by heavy footsteps, slowly drifting away into the gloom shadows.

Arthur was driving to Susan's apartment to pick her up for their date. He had made reservations at another fashionable club but he was not too eager to get there. It was always too crowded for his taste. Susan had asked him to make the reservations and Arthur did not want to disappoint her.

"Hi! I haven't kept you waiting?"

"Why? Do I look impatient?" Arthur kissed Susan, who just got in the car and leaned her body towards him.

When they got to their table and had a drink, Susan started talking about her experience with the pervert's phone call.

"How do you know it was a pervert?"

"He kept doing those strange noises and he didn't say a word..."

"Don't worry about it Susan. Those things happen quite often."

"Who says I'm worried? I'm just upset he got me out of my hot tab..."

"Getting beautiful for me, Suz?"

"A girl can only try..."

Arthur pulled her gently towards him, across the table, and kissed her.

Susan was drinking her vodka when the tall stranger approached her table, pulled out a chair and sat down, offering Susan a glass of champagne. Arthur had just gone to the men's room. Susan was looking at the man with astonished eyes and was unable to say anything. The man was quite drunk.

"Can I offer you a drink baby?"

"Please sir, I'm with someone..."

"So ….what ? ” the man leaned against the table, trying to kiss Susan.

Susan pulled away and was surprised to see at the stranger's face a terrible expression of agony. Arthur was behind him and he was twisting his arm in a very painful way.

"The lady is with me, if you don't mind sir..." Arthur said in a cold way.

The man dropped on the floor in terrible pain, and dead drunk.

Arthur and Susan had not exchanged many words after the incident at the club. They were in Arthur's car, heading back to Susan's apartment. Susan was looking at him, unable to believe that Arthur could become violent. She was pleased to watch him defending her from the drunken man but she hadn't realised all the time they were going out together that he had a violent side. A part of her was frightened of him, even though she tried to assure herself of being silly. When Arthur asked her if he could join her at her apartment she said that she had a headache. For the first time, the attraction she always felt about him simply was not there. She kept remembering the coldness of his eyes, while he was hurting the man who tried to approach her. Those were not the eyes of the man she felt so close. The darkness that came out of this made her shiver.

5

The girl's skin was being ripped open with a shiny razor and the dark red, warm blood was pouring out of the freshly cut veins and down the woman's shoulders, forming a small pond on the cracked pavement. The victim was not yet unconscious and was able to watch her attacker's gloved hands placing the razor against her chest, and slowly tearing out her skin, with careful moves, like performing a ritual. The pain and the terrible agony, soon gave way to a peaceful acceptance of death which she felt that was about to come. In a few seconds she passed out.

Susan was taking her dress off and was ready to go to bed when she heard a noise in the living room. She shivered, and grabbed a pair of scissors, which were lying next to the mirror. She slowly walked to the living room, holding her breath, and keeping the scissors pointed out in front of her.

"Is anyone there, I'm warning you..."

Susan heard nothing when she got into the living room and saw nothing when she hit the light switch. She dropped her body on the sofa, really frightened, and still holding on to the scissors.

"I'm going to call Arthur and ask him to come over. It was a mistake to send him away in the first place."

Susan tried Arthur's cell but nobody answered.

Susan kept calling, feeling unable to text him. She was in a terrible state and wanted to hear his voice.

"Yes..."

"Arthur, are you still on the road ?... Could you come over. You wouldn't believe what just happened..."

"Susan, baby, what's the matter? You sound upset..."

"Somebody was here. I'm so frightened. I was ready to go to bed..."

"Are you all right?"

"Yes but come on over, please..."

"Sure, I'll be right there. Don't worry, it was probably you imagination."

"No, it was real footsteps..."

"OK baby, I'm coming over. Try to relax.”

Arthur and Susan spent the night together and in the morning they both drove to the office in Arthur's car. Susan was not frightened any more but she still asked Arthur to spend the following night with her, just to make her feel better with the thought of someone else being around the house.

It was about twelve-thirty when Susan was walking to her favourite downtown restaurant to have her lunch. She was going alone.   Arthur was too busy with the new deal with the American company and could not join her. She was walking in a very busy city street but still she had the impression that somebody was following her. The other night's experience came to her mind and she started walking quickly. She turned and looked back a couple of times but she was not able to spot anyone following her. She hurried to the restaurant where she had a terrible lunch, looking anxiously out of the restaurant's windows, watching everybody and searching for anyone who looked suspicious.

"Suz, you look worried. What's the matter?"

Arthur asked Susan when he saw her stepping into his office, returning from her lunch break.

"I don't know Arthur. First it was the pervert's phone call. Then the noises in the living room last night. Today, I thought someone was following me but when I looked, I didn't see anyone."

"Baby don't worry. You are tired. That's all. Maybe you need a vacation..."

"No Arthur. I'm sure. Somebody's after me."

"Now, now Susan... what are you talking about? That's nonsense."

"No it's not... I don't know... Arthur what am I going to do?" Susan rushed into Arthur's open arms, and started crying over his shoulder.

"Now, now baby, don't cry. We'll work something out. I was talking with Charley last week. He knows this Dr.Peters. I hear he is very good. He helped Charley with a problem he had with his job..."

"I don't need a shrink Arthur, I'm not crazy and I'm not making things up..."

"Of course not baby. You will only talk to him."

Arthur finally convinced Susan to go and see a psychiatrist. She discussed with him the threatening situations which she experienced. Dr.Peters was a very understanding man and advised her to go to the police if that sort of thing happened again, provided she had proof that her life was really in danger.

"The experiences you had so far cannot be described as threatening," Dr.Peters explained. "In all cases you saw nothing, you only heard noises."

"And finally," Dr.Peters concluded, "without wanting to insult you Susan, work stress and pressure at the office often makes people exaggerate situations, which in other cases are almost self-explanatory, such as noises in the night which turn out to be the neighbour's cat."

Dr.Peters gave Susan a prescription for sleeping pills and walked her to the door.

Susan was partly relieved of her anxiety after seeing Dr.Peters but still was not quite comfortable with the idea of staying home alone during the night. Unfortunately, Arthur had to go on a sudden business trip to New York and could not spend the next three nights with her.

It was the first time since she met Arthur that her sense of independence, that so proudly promoted to her girlfriends when she was talking about her relationship, now seemed as mere loneliness and despair.

6

The red, shinning sports car pulled into the dark garage and parked next to a silver sedan. The tall blond girl walked out of the car. She was dressed in a tight black evening dress. She switched on the car alarm and walked to the elevator doors. The sound of her high heels, thumping on the cement floor, could be heard clearly across the empty garage.

A man came out of the shadows and stood in front of her.

"Oh... It's you, you startled me! What are you doing here this late at night?"

The man was still standing in front of the young woman without saying a word.

"We haven't seen each other for a while," the woman went on talking, "is something wrong?", she added noticing the expression on his face.

The man suddenly pulled out a large razor, and violently pushed the woman to the floor. He stuffed a piece of cloth in her mouth and started slowly to tear out the skin of her face with the razor.

The girl felt the cold blade on her cheeks and sensed that this must be the end. She desperately tried to push away her attacker. She kicked him and hit him on his back. But the man did not stop. He kept cutting her skin until she could no longer see the man's face, with her own blood dripping into her eyes.

The phone was ringing in Susan's apartment as she opened the door, her hands full with groceries. She run to the land line and lifted the receiver.

A friend whom she haven't seen for years was in town. He was there on business and wanted to see her for old times' sake. Arthur was not in town and Susan was not comfortable with the idea of staying in her apartment alone. She rarely went out with other men, but this was a time of fear and uncertainty.

Susan and her old friend John had dinner and talked about old times. When John drove Susan back home she asked him to come up for a drink.

"But I thought you and Arthur are pretty close..."

"We are! I just asked you for a drink John. I don't like staying alone in my place after what happened. I told you about it at the restaurant."

"Sure, I understand. I'll stay with you as long as you like, if this is gonna make you feel better."

"Thanks! I owe you one!"

It was way past midnight when Susan kissed John good night at her front door. She took a sleeping pill and went to bed. Before going to sleep, Susan switched on the television to catch the late news.

"The razor killer stroke again..." Susan came out of the bathroom and turned up the volume.

"The girl was found in a garage two hours ago. Helen Bates, 23, is the razor killer's seventh victim..."

Susan could no longer understand what the newscaster was saying after hearing the victim's name. She felt a sudden chill down her spine and laid still, watching the television, completely motionless.   Helen was her best friend. They knew each other since high school and they were very close.

"I was talking to her only yesterday... She was going away for the weekend and she was so happy... When will they catch that maniac..?" Susan threw herself on the bed and started crying.

The next day, Susan tried to reach Arthur on the telephone and ask him to come back. She didn't manage to contact with him and she felt very frightened. Now, after her friend's death, she was almost certain that the razor killer was after her and that she was about to become his next victim. Susan decided to call Dr. Peters and set up a session with him.

"Susan, I can assure you that nobody is trying to harm you. Your friend's death was purely a coincidence." Dr. Peters tried to calm her down.

"However, I am not very happy to discover that your ideas about somebody trying to hurt you have now become an obsession and are focused on the razor killer. The razor killer **is** a real threat and you should avoid wandering about alone at night, but try to think about it rationally. The killer is a maniac who kills at random. He couldn't possibly be after **you** as a person, as Susan Faithwell."

Susan left Dr. Peters' office and headed to the elevator. The session had no positive effect on her disturbed nerves and her anxiety was continuously increasing.

The elevator stopped at the 12th floor and the doors opened. A man, wearing a ski mask and a dark overcoat walked into the elevator. Susan's hands became numb and cold of anxiety and fear. The man was also wearing dark glasses and Susan could not see his eyes but she was certain that he was staring at her all the way down to the ground floor. When the doors opened Susan almost run out and hurried to her car. She turned on the ignition and looked at the rear view mirror. The man with the ski mask was standing in front of the building and was looking at the street traffic. Susan did not gave him a second look and accelerated away.

She drove around the neighbourhood for a while and when she was sure that nobody was following her, she drove back home.

7

Susan tried to reach Arthur on the telephone for another time but she failed again. She was desperate for someone to be with her. She was too frightened to stay alone and she called her friend John with whom she had dinner the other night. He asked him to come over and keep her company.

"Of course Susan, I'm on my way. What do you think friends are for?"

The door bell rang half an hour later. As Susan was opening the door, the man behind it put a ski mask in his overcoat pocket and wiped the sweat off his face.

"Hello John, I'm so relieved now that you are here…"

They both went inside and Susan closed the door.

The janitor was walking down the hall way and towards the small room where he changed his clothes before work. The office building was too big for just an old man to handle, but she was not complaining. The company administration was making a lot of cuts in expenses lately, and as retirement was only one year and a half away he didn't want to take any chances. He put his key in the lock and turned it, but the door was already open. The old janitor was puzzled and paused for a few seconds before reaching for the light switch, as he felt that he was stepping on wet floor. When he finally turned the lights on and looked inside the room the keys dropped from his hands and he shivered. The young woman was lying at the end of the room, facing the floor. Her skin was not visible as blood covered her entire body. Her clothes were torn to pieces and thrown next to her. The old janitor went closer with shaking steps, and realised that the woman had no skin left on her body. It had been torn apart, leaving her flesh exposed, and dripping with blood.

Back in Susan's apartment, a few minutes later, Susan was talking with John when she noticed something hanging out of his overcoat pocket.

"What's that John?"

"Oh, it's my ski mask. I always wear it when it is cold."

"Let me see that..." Susan remembered the man with the ski mask in the elevator, when she left Dr. Peters' office earlier that day.

John put on the ski mask and started laughing, "How about it, Susan, do you like it?"

Susan recognised the same ski mask with the man in the elevator.

Arthur was driving to Susan's apartment. He had a compelling urge to see her. He was tired and stressed. Business worried him a lot lately and he was on some heavy tranquillisers. The doctor who subscribed him the pills had specifically ordered not to take more than one per day. Arthur violated the instructions because of work stress becoming too unbearable to handle. In addition to that, for the past few days, he was under the impression that he was forgetting things. He blamed those symptoms to the pills and kept promising to himself that he will not take them again. However, he kept breaking his promise. He also thought that the pills were to blame for some bad dreams and disturbing thoughts he had been having for the last few days. He could not explain them in any other way.

Arthur turned on the car radio to listen to some music trying to clear away the unpleasant thoughts, that kept coming once again.

"...In other news, the razor killer's latest victim has been discovered by an old janitor late last night. It is the third in the last two days and the eighth in a row. The police seems unable to trace the serial killer who leaves no traces, and became too busy during the past few days..."

Arthur quickly turned off the radio. The news made the unpleasant thoughts come back to his mind, however hard he tried to push them away.

Meanwhile, Susan had politely asked John to leave. She told him that she was feeling better and that she wanted to get some sleep. However, the true reason was, that she felt frightened when she saw his ski mask. She kept telling to herself that she was being silly, but still, she sent John away.

She closed the door and secured all the safety locks.

Then she stood behind the door for a while and watched her hands trembling. Susan could not control them.

Suddenly, the door bell rang.

"John, did you forget something?"

Susan opened the door, facing a man with a ski mask, the same one that John had on, the same one with the man at the elevator.

Susan noticed in terror, that the man was holding a razor, covered with blood. She didn't have time to scream, as he stuffed a dirty cloth into her mouth and pushed her inside the house.

John was lying on the elevator floor, in terrible pain, facing down, and trying desperately to stop the blood which was spraying its way out of his stomach and all over the elevator. The man had entered the elevator when the doors opened at the ground floor. John was certain that he had seen him before, but he didn't have the chance to take a good look at him as he stabbed him in the stomach, just a few seconds after the doors opened. John was still alive, and fought with all his strength not to loose consciousness. He knew that this would mean the end. He tried to raise his arm and push the button for Susan's floor. Susan was fighting with her attacker, but he was too strong for her. The hand with the razor was coming closer to her face. The young woman desperately tried to push him away. A spontaneous cry of fear came out of her mouth,

"*Arthur...* Help!..."

The hand with the razor remained in the air, pointing at her but the man stopped pushing Susan down on the floor. He was just sitting there, looking at her. Susan reached out for the razor and as she pushed it away, it ripped open the man's ski mask. When she saw the man's face, she froze to death and remained motionless. The man tried to grasp the razor, which was dropped on the carpet but a hand, covered with blood, took a hold of the razor first. John, with all his remaining strength, raised the blade and pushed it into the man's neck.

A terrible cry of agony came out of Arthur's mouth and he dropped on the floor dead, eyes open, facing the ceiling, dark, warm blood coming out of his mouth, dripping down his chin, and on the carpet, under his head. He laid there motionless, his eyes fading to oblivion.

8

"Arthur had a double personality, he led two entirely different lives, he was two different people, one having absolutely no knowledge of the other's existence. Most of the time he was Arthur Twines, the respectable marketing executive, but on other occasions he became the razor killer, murdering innocent young women."

Susan was sitting next to John's bed at the hospital. He had suffered a severe injury, but a month after his operation he was better, and able to talk again. They were both listening to the doctor, who was explaining them what happened.

"But doctor," John asked "why did he attack **me**?..."

"He saw you as a threat to Susan and in his sick way he tried to protect her. You see John, Arthur was aware that you and Susan knew each other. At the time he was coming to Susan's apartment he must had experienced a moment of epiphany, realising in a way his double personality. Mixed emotions, emerging in his troubled mind, interacted upon his two personalities. As Susan's boyfriend, he was jealous of you, and as a maniac killer he tried to murder you to protect her, with the only intention to kill her himself, immediately afterwards. You are both very lucky to be alive."

Susan burst into tears and the doctor tried to comfort her.

"Doctor, can you please leave us alone for a minute?" John asked.

"Of course, but keep it short. Remember, you should both avoid overexcitement."

John took Susan's hand and held it. The doctor left the room and closed the door behind him.